For Esmé
B.F.

Fun-to-Read Picture Books have been grouped into three approximate readability levels by Bernice and Cliff Moon. Yellow books are suitable for beginners; red books for readers acquiring first fluency; blue books for more advanced readers.

This book has been assessed as Stage 8 according to *Individualised Reading*, by Bernice and Cliff Moon, published by The Centre for the Teaching of Reading, University of Reading School of Education.

This poem was first published in Charles Causley's *Figgie Hobbin* (Macmillan, 1970).

This edition first published 1986 by Walker Books Ltd 184-192 Drummond Street London NW1 3HP

Text © 1970 Charles Causley Illustrations © 1986 Barbara Firth

First printed 1986 Printed and bound by L.E.G.O., Vicenza, Italy

British Library Cataloguing in Publication Data Causley, Charles 'Quack!' said the billy-goat. – (Fun-to-read picture books) I. Title II. Firth, Barbara III. Series 823'.914[J]   PZ7

ISBN 0-7445-0479-1

'Quack!'
said the billy-goat

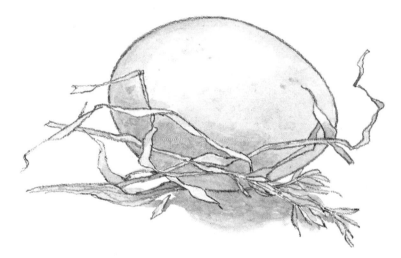

WRITTEN BY
Charles Causley

ILLUSTRATED BY
Barbara Firth

WALKER BOOKS
LONDON

'Quack!' said the billy-goat.

'Oink!' said the hen.

'Miaow!' said the little chick
running in the pen.

'Hobble-gobble!' said the dog.

'Cluck!' said the sow.

'Tu-whit tu-whoo!' the donkey said.

'Baa!' said the cow.

'Hee-haw!' the turkey cried.

The duck began to moo.

All at once the sheep went,

'Cock-a-doodle-doo!'

The owl coughed and
cleared his throat
and he began to bleat.
'Bow-wow!' said the cock
swimming in the leat.

'Cheep-cheep!' said the cat
as she began to fly.

'Farmer's been and laid an egg –

that's the reason why.'